F

JJ
Cassels
Older
18.95

We hurried to Uncle David's mansion, expecting to see twelve paintings. There must have been a hundred!

Dad sighed, "How will we ever unravel the mystery?"

I knew the answer! "Remember what Uncle's letter said, 'Look on the backs of the paintings!' Dad, that's where all the clues will be, the dates and the names and addresses! We can figure out whom the paintings belong to and where to send them, then find out what became of Uncle David."

That's exactly what we did, and so can you! You will see, once we found the first painting, Uncle's story began.

M. Goose
1697 Rue Perrault
Paris, France

Dr. David Harleyson
38 Tamworth Lane
Philadelphia, PA, USA

Saturday, 1 January

Dearest David,

Happy New Year!
I have been busy. Every morning I'm at my desk, writing down little rhymes about our friends. In the afternoons, I walk to the corner café for a sandwich and tea. The children come running to me, and sing, "Oh, please tell us a story!" They climb onto my lap, all smiles. It is so delightful. I love them all!

Your news is so exciting! I am so pleased you will be coming to Paris. Please tell me you will finally have the time to paint my portrait! So many of our friends want their portraits painted. Plan on being busy with your paints and brushes.

I'll meet you at the train station on January 12 at 3:00. I have the guest room all ready for you, and you are most welcome to stay as long as you please.

Fond regards, M. Goose

P.S. Sir Wolfe has a new play opening in Brussels, February 12.
He's expecting you to be there.

THE GREAT ATLANTIC COMPANY

NEW YORK HARBOR
TO
LE HAVRE, FRANCE
DEPARTS: DOCK A
JANUARY 5
6:00 A.M.

OCEAN WAVES HAVE YOU ILL?
TAKE DR. FOSTER'S LITTLE PILL!

DR. FOSTER * near Gloucester

Continental Railroad
Le Havre, France
to Paris, France

DEPARTS: 12 JANUARY   6:00 A.M.
ARRIVES: 12 JANUARY   3:00 P.M.
SLEEPER CAR # S42

A Walk in the Woods

A Play in Three Acts

Written, Acted, and Directed by

Sir Harry Le Wolfe

Starring Betsy Lambkin, as

Little Red Riding Hood

Opening

Saturday, 12 February

eight o'clock

Sir Harry Le Wolfe
55 Aesop Street
Brussels, Belgium

2 February

Dear David,

Thank you for offering to paint my portrait! I know you will see me for the intelligent, generous, kindhearted, handsome, and modest being that I am—nothing like the big, bad wolf in my plays.

I am already writing my next play. It will be entitled THREE PIGS or THREE LITTLE PIGS. Please consider taking the lead role! You would be perfect!

In friendship, Harry

DIRECTOR'S PASS

A Walk in the Woods

Dr. David Harleyson

Opening night * 8:00

Front row * center seat

Harry

Continental Railroad

Brussels, Belgium, to Copenhagen, Denmark

DEPARTS: 28 FEBRUARY   8:00 A.M.

ARRIVES: 30 FEBRUARY   12:00 P.M.

Frog Prince's Party!

The Times Gazette

BRUSSELS: The opening-night crowd gave a standing ovation—crying "Wolfe! Wolfe!"—when the final curtain fell on *A Walk in the Woods.* When asked, "Why did you make it such a big production?" Sir Wolfe said, "All the better to entertain you with, my dear!"

Famous artist Dr. David Harleyson was in the audience. He has turned down a starring role in Sir Wolfe's next play, *Three Pigs,* saying he knows nothing of house building or of acting; he is just a painter.

Waving to the crowd, Harry, David, and Betsy left for a late-night supper at a restaurant popular with

DENMARK TIMES
COPENHAGEN SOCIETY PAGE NEWS

Saturday, 5 March

The King's Very Fancy Spring Dinner Party, held last night, was to honor the princess and her frog prince. Among the many special guests were two Americans: **Dr. David Harleyson,** a famous artist, and **Miss Lill Pigg,** an opera star. It was a glittering evening, with all the ladies in long dresses and the gentlemen in black tuxedos. Musicians played and candles shimmered. Delicious aromas filled the air. Gold-trimmed plates, filled with the most sumptuous delicacies, were set before each lady and gentleman. Everyone was most polite, saying their thank-yous and pleases in soft voices.

The surprise of the evening came when the prince shot out his tongue and caught a fly—right in front of the princess! Then he swallowed it! In the shocked silence that followed, a small "Ouch!" was heard. Miss Pigg covered a giggle with her napkin. This reporter was told the princess had kicked the prince, just as hard as she could, in his royal shin, under the royal table, with her tiny royal toe!

The king then bellowed for the musicians to play and ordered the candles to shimmer! A certain two Americans spent the rest of the evening talking with each other. The evening was a great success.

Miss Lill Pigg
Table 3

By Order of the King
Your presence is requested

4 March   Half past five in the evening
* Very Dress-Up * No Bare Feet *

* Hans C. Andersen Drive *   * Copenhagen * Denmark *

Star light,
Star bright,
First star
I see tonight,
I wish I may,
I wish I might,
Have the wish
I wish tonight.

I. B. Spider
4 Warp Weft Lane
Bremen, Germany

Dr. David Harleyson
c/o The Frog Prince
Copenhagen,
Denmark

Dear David,
It will be a delight to see you again. I am certain your painting of me will be perfect. And I do promise to sit still.

Love, itsy bitsy

April 1

THE SITUATION HERE HAS BEEN IMPOSSIBLE!
Every day it has rained! The roof leaks from the waterspout!
Every morning I paint Miss Spider's portrait. Every afternoon,
down comes the rain and washes the portrait out. THEN out
comes the sun, dries up all the rain, and Miss Spider and I start
up to paint again.
I'LL NEVER BE FINISHED!!!
RAIN, RAIN GO AWAY!!
COME AGAIN SOME OTHER DAY!!

GRETEL'S ART SHOP

1 April

One . . . teensy-weensy canvas
One . . . small brush
One . . . very small brush
One . . . itsy-bitsy brush!

One, two, "I'd like some glue,"
Three, four, "It's by the door."
Five, six, "And pastel sticks."
Seven, eight, "They must be
straight!"
Nine, ten, "Come back again!"

PARIS
10·4

M. Goose
1697 Rue Perrault
Paris, France

Dr. David Harleyson
c/o I. B. Spider
4 Warp Weft Lane
Bremen, Germany

I. B. Spider 4 Weft Warp Lane Bremen, Germany

Dearest David,
Thank You! My painting is ever so
beautiful. You were so kind and patient to be
able to finish it under such difficulties. Your
stories of the prince eating the fly were so very
funny, but really, they did make me hungry!
Please send the painting to me as quickly as
you are able, I want all my friends to see it.
Much love,
itsy bitsy

19 April, Tuesday

Dearest David,
    A dear American friend has come to stay with
me. She is in rehearsal with The Opera Company.
I am having a big gala dinner party for her.
        * Sunday, May 1, at 6:00 *
You are invited! Wear your tuxedo!

M. Goose

Continental Railroad

Bremen, Germany, to Paris, France

DEPARTS:	29 APRIL	7:00 A.M.
ARRIVES:	30 APRIL	2:00 P.M.

SLEEPER CAR #A31 • DINING CAR

2 May, Monday

Dearest David,

So you didn't mind my little party after all. I wish you could have seen your face when Miss Lill walked in! What a surprise!

You should know, she has talked of no one but you since the royal supper, and she still giggles about the prince swallowing that silly fly!

I am so pleased you have decided to paint her portrait. It means you two will be here in Paris for a while.

Fondly, M. Goose

Café Américain
Paris

2 Coffees with cream & sugar
2 Pancake specials with s—

20 May

Café Les Bon Temps

Lunch--11:00-2:00

1 Watercress sandwich
2 Tomato, cucumber sandwiches
2 Iced teas
4 Chocolate-chip cookies
2 Chocolate ice creams

Fr 100c Total

May 30

Dearest David,

I very much enjoyed all those hours we spent walking together through the park, talking and laughing. It was really quite lovely.

I wondered how you managed to have enough time to paint, but my portrait is beautiful!

Now that rehearsals are beginning, I will be busy every minute. Still, I will miss you when you leave for Switzerland. Please give my regards to dear Ant and Grasshopper.

Fondly, Lill

FAY'S FLOWERS

31 May

Two dozen red roses

Deliver to:
Miss Lill Pigg
c/o M. Goose
1697 Rue Perrault
Paris

CAFÉ DE LA TOUR EIFFEL

2 Onion Soups
2 Truffle Omelets
2 Asparagus Soufflés
2 Turnip Salads & Rolls
2 Coffees with Cream
2 Chocolate Cakes with lots of fudge sauce

Total Fr 250 c
May 30

PARIS, FRANCE, TO
HINZEL, SWITZERLAND

1 June, Wednesday * 9:00 a.m.
One passenger
First class * All the way *

Reservations by:
HEIDI TRAVEL

Wednesday, June 29   Hinzel, Switzerland

What a pair!

Ant works nonstop gathering seeds and [stores] them away for the winter. Grasshopper just pl[ays] and plays. When Ant complains, Grasshopper says, "It's the middle of summer, the day is beautiful, don't worry, be happy!"

Ant laughs, "I am happy, but I think this winter you will be dancing for your supper!" I love them both!

Their painting is finished, and in the morning I'm off to Amsterdam and Miss Lill.

Owl, Esq.
1812 Amstel
Amsterdam, Netherlands

AMSTERDAM
15·06
NEDERLAND

June 15
Amsterdam, Netherlands

***************FROM THE DESK OF OWL *****************

Dear Friend David,

Pussycat and I are so excited to have you staying with us in July! It's been many years since you and I met in the Bong Tree Woods, where you gave me your nose ring for my wedding day. Now you will be painting our portrait! Wonderful! Our guest room is yours. Please plan on staying with us.

We look forward to meeting your friend Miss Lill Pigg. How exciting that the opening night of the opera will be here! We have our front-row tickets, thank you! We will be bringing red roses for Miss Lill.

Your friend,

Owl

(musical notation)

July 30

Amsterdam

Dear David,
    You, Owl, and Pussycat have made this a wonderful July!
    This Lill Pigg went to market   [we always bought flowers]
    This Lill Pigg stayed home   [we four played cards]
    This Lill Pigg ate baked apples   [we celebrated at Rembrandt's]
    This Lill Pigg had none   [thank you, but no sliced quince for me!]
    And now, this Lill Pigg will be thinking of we, we, we, all the way home!
I'm writing this on the morning train, off with The Opera Company to Paris.
M. Goose has asked me to please stay with her again.
I had a wonderful time, David. Thank you.
                Love, Lill

*************************FROM THE DESK OF OWL******************

Sunday, July 31
Amsterdam, Netherlands

Dear David,
    Please send me the cleaning bill for your suit and Miss Lill's dress. Pussycat tells me I looked pretty funny with both feet in the air, and my small guitar in hand, as the boat flipped over. My beautiful pea-green boat! Standing and singing seemed like such a good idea. At least the water was warm, and we were all laughing!
    Our portrait is wonderful and ever so elegant. As soon as it has been framed please send it quickly! Thank you! It was so pleasant having you here and meeting your friend Miss Lill. I hope your trip to Norway goes well. Please give our best to the Gruff Brothers.

        Your friend, Owl

TELEGRAM

31 JULY stop DR. DAVID HARLEYSON stop WILL MEET YOU 8PM AUGUST 5 AT THE OSLO TRAIN STATION stop SINCERELY WILLIAM G. GRUFF stop OSLO stop

Friday, August 26

TRIP, TRAP, TRIP, TRAP, TRIP, TRAP, TRIP

Those three brothers never stop!

Back and forth, back and forth, over the bridge!

No wonder that old troll was so grumpy!

I've finished Billy's portrait. They all love it.

Wednesday the four of us are taking off for England.

Our old friend Hare is in a footrace with Tortoise,

and we want to be there! I'm still hoping...

Miss Lill...

at the ra...

GRUFF BROTHERS

* MOWING *
* LANDSCAPING *

38 GREENHILLS ROAD
OSLO, NORWAY

August 27, Saturday

Dear David,

I'm terribly sorry I can't join you. The Opera Company is in the middle of a disaster! Our next show is opening soon. We must practice! Together! But now the entire chorus of twenty-four blackbirds have quit! Gone! Flown off! They are going to sing for the king! We are all furious! I hope they all get baked into a pie!

I miss you. Please write.

Fondly, Lill

VIKING STEAMSHIP CO.

OSLO, NORWAY, TO
SOUTHAMPTON, ENGLAND

31 AUGUST   7:00 A.M.
4 PASSENGERS / FIRST CLASS
BOARDING AT 6:00

PAID IN FULL

Oslo Photo Studio

LONDON NEWS
HARE WINS!

LONDON: 4 Sept. — **Hare** is so far out in front, by far the faster runner, that the *London News* declares he will be the easy winner. Hare has long boasted of his speed, but **Tortoise** isn't bothered. He just keeps on going. Tortoise and Hare got off ____ but Hare quickly lef____

LONDON NEWS
SURPRISE WINNER!

LONDON: 5 Sept. — The *London News* made a mistake! **Tortoise** is the winner! **Hare** was so certain he would win, he stopped to take a nap before he crossed the finish line. He was seen out late the night before with **Dr. David Harleyson** and the three **Gruff** brothers. Tortoise stayed home and got a good night's sleep. Hare tells us that he has learned an important lesson from this surpri____ events. He and ____

Slow and Steady Wins the Race!

"I'm not very fast, but I keep on going," says Tortoise. "I guess he caught me napping!" Hare admitted. The runners shook hands, and Hare offered his congratulations. After signing autographs, Hare, Tortoise, the three Gruffs, and Dr. David Harleyson left for a big lunch at the Blue Lion Inn. Tortoise smiled and waved to the cheering crowd. It's all part ____ ____ to the occasion

DEAR DAVID,
PLEASE FIX THE PAINTING
I LOOK TOO SMALL!!!
THANK YOU, Grizz

Dearest David,
I hope you can fix the painting.
I look much too BIG!
Thank you, dear.
Love
Ursula

Dear Uncle David,
We all enjoyed your company.
I think the painting is just right!
Thank you for my storybook!
Love, Little Grizell

M. Goose
1697 Rue Perrault
Paris, France

Monday, 24 October
Dearest David,
Your thank-you letter arrived. You are most welcome! It was a pleasure to have you here. I hope you are not imposing on the three bears too much, eating all their porridge, etc. And now you are on your way to Scotland to see dear Baa Baa, then home to America. I will miss you.
Did you know D. Diddle will be performing, 30 December, in your hometown, Philadelphia? Her fiddle playing is magical. I am sending you a ticket. It will be waiting for you when you get home. I'm certain you will enjoy the evening!
Much love, M. Goose

British Rail
Cardiff, Wales, to
Glasgow, Scotland
DEPARTS: 31 OCTOBER   8:00 P.M.
ARRIVES: 1 NOVEMBER   10:00 A.M.
SLEEPER CAR # A22 • FIRST CLASS

24 November, Thursday

Baa Baa
72 Upthelane
Glasgow, Scotland

My Dear David,

It will be cold on your voyage home! Please take this wool

sweater to keep you warm. (Don't worry, I have three bags full!) Yes, sir!

Yes, sir! Here every master and dame is wearing one of my knitted creations.

I'll tell you a secret. I save the softest sweaters, with the best colors, to

give to the little boys and girls that live down the lane. They always give

me a big smile and a warm hug and say, "Thank you, Baa Baa!"

David, I love my portrait! Please hurry with the framing and get it

back to me. Thank you, dear. Have a safe journey!

Love,

Baa Baa

An extra
button!
B. B.

Crossing the
Atlantic in
my new
Sweater

THE
GREAT
ATLANTIC
COMPANY

GREENOCK, SCOTLAND
TO
NEW YORK HARBOR
28 NOVEMBER
9:00 A.M.
FIRST CLASS

There, behind us, was
Uncle David's self-portrait!
"Dad, I think we have to
look behind that painting, too!"
This is what we found . . .

December 31

Dear Brother and Nephew,

Now that you have found all twelve paintings and have them in order, you know how Miss Lill Pigg and I met. When she left Amsterdam in July, I thought I might never see her again. Then, last night, in the theater, we were sitting side by side. Dear, romantic Mother Goose had given Miss Lill a ticket, too! After the show, under a starry sky, Lill and I took a carriage ride through the park. When I asked her to marry me, she said yes!

Early tomorrow we are leaving for Tobago, to plan our wedding. Your invitation and your tickets for the trip are in my desk drawer. **Please do come! We want you to be there!**

Much love, *David*

P.S. Please do send the paintings, they are expected. The shipping has all been prepaid. Thank you!

* Your Presence Is Requested As *
DR. DAVID HARLEYSON
and
MISS LILL PIGG

Join in Marriage
February 14, at 6:00 p.m.

Hand in hand, at the edge of the sand.
All by the light of the moon, the moon.

The Caribbean Line

Passengers:
Master John D. Harleyson
Mr. Michael Harleyson
First Class * Upper Deck
* PAID *

New York Harbor
to
Tobago, West Indies
Departing: February 5

To
Timothy Travaglini, Craig S. Hood, and especially to
John D. Harleyson for sharing with me memories of his famous uncle

Special thanks to the following for sitting so patiently for their portraits:
• Mother Goose • the Big, Bad Wolf • the Frog Prince • the Itsy Bitsy Spider •
• this Lill Pig • the Ant and the Grasshopper • the Owl and the Pussycat •
• one Billy Goat Gruff • the Tortoise and the Hare • the Three Bears •
• Baa Baa Black Sheep • the Cat (and the Fiddle) •

First published in the United States of America in 2004 by Walker Publishing Company, Inc.

Published simultaneously in Canada by Fitzhenry and Whiteside, Markham, Ontario L3R 4T8

For information about permission to reproduce selections from this book, write to Permissions,
Walker & Company, 104 Fifth Avenue, New York, New York 10011

Library of Congress Cataloging-in-Publication Data

Cassels, Jean.
The mysterious collection of Dr. David Harleyson / Jean Cassels.
p. cm.
Summary: When a world famous artist disappears, his nephew pieces together the clues found on the backs of a group of portraits, which feature characters from Mother Goose, Grimm, and Aesop, to decipher where the artist went and where to send the pictures.
ISBN 0-8027-8916-1 (HC) — ISBN 0-8027-8918-8 (RE)
[1. Portraits—Fiction. 2. Artists—Fiction. 3. Characters in literature—Fiction. 4. Animals—Fiction. 5. Letters—Fiction.
6. Mystery and detective stories.] I. Title

PZ7.C268525My 2004
[Fic]—dc22   2003066564

The artist used gouache on 140-pound Arches hot press 100-percent rag watercolor paper to create the illustrations for this book.

Book design by Victoria Allen

Visit Walker & Company's Web site at www.walkeryoungreaders.com

Printed in Hong Kong

2 4 6 8 10 9 7 5 3 1